THE DEAD OAK

THE DEAD OAK

By Marvin Visher

Short Stuff Publishing

Copyright © 2016 By Marvin Visher

Book Design by Misty D. Billman
Cover Design by Melissa Johnson

Printed in the United States of America

First Printing, 2016

ISBN 978-0-9899364-6-0

Short Stuff Publishing L.L.C.

Aurora, CO 80011

Other Books By Short Stuff Publishing

The Prophecy of Kalodorim

REVELATIONS (Book One)
DISCIPLES (Book Two) *Coming soon.*
UNTITLED (Book Three) *Coming soon*

The Hisime Ara Chronicles

Royal Elves (Book One)
The Pit (Book Two)
Old Mine (Book Three)

To my wife Misty, the enforcer of dreams

PROLOGUE

"Fuck you, you old hag!" roared the man. "You couldn't turn a pocket today if your life depended on it!" Lightning flashed through the dirty windows and across the moth-eaten curtains. She threw a chipped tea cup at him—the cup smashing against the moldy flower print wallpaper.

The house had once been new and well-kept, but that was before the current owners took residence there. Now everything stunk of rot and disuse. From the cobwebbed ceiling fan to the threadbare carpet, the entire house spoke of apathy and negligence.

She screamed incoherently at him. They had been fighting for hours now. Any semblance of the issue that started it all had long since been discarded as the fight escalated beyond reason. If anyone knew that the fight started over who ate the last piece of bacon this morning, they would have laughed at the incredulity of it.

Any thoughts that the neighbors might call the police were disregarded—the neighbors had long since become deaf to the yelling and tearing they heard most nights. The police had been called several times to break up their fights in the past, but since neither the old woman nor her husband would ever press charges, they always released them. Now whenever the fighting and screaming was particularly bad, the neighbors merely shut the windows, they knew calling the police was a waste.

Tonight was one of those nights—all the neighbors had shut their windows up hours ago. The oncoming storm aided in drowning out the noise and the neighborhood was grateful for that.

Thunder rumbled through the house as a chair flew through the dining room and struck the light fixture hanging above. The light shattered, plunging the room into darkness; lit briefly by flashes of lightning. To an onlooker, it would have seemed like quite a feat of strength for such a decrepit old woman to throw that chair but the couple fighting in the dingy room were not all that old. The onlooker might be surprised to learn that the couple were actually only in their late forties—though they appeared much older. Smoking, meth, cocaine, and poor hygiene had taken its toll.

The old man dodged the chair in the nick of time as it tumbled into pieces on the floor, save for one leg that went through the drywall.

"What are you trying to do, kill me?!" he exclaimed.

"If only I could be so lucky!" the woman spat reaching for another chair.

"You crazy bitch!" he screamed, jumping over the broken chair now at his feet. He began to chase her around the house.

More items were knocked off the walls and tables and the sound of porcelain breaking, vases toppling off of stands, end tables crashing to the ground could be heard through the neighborhood. No picture frames broke—there were no pictures to break. In fact, their house was completely devoid of anything with sentimental value. Most of what fell to the floor, or was thrown through the halls, were relics from a life spent fleecing and manipulating others; rings and broaches from old successful women, paintings from men who had long ago grown old, tokens of affection from men whose vanity overcame their senses. Most of it was worthless now. Anything of value had long ago been pawned or sold.

They rounded the bed in her room; her grabbing objects and flinging them back at him and him dodging and roaring at her. Lightning flashed and thunder boomed to punctuate their mad race through the house. They dashed across the hall and went into his room. The man caught a book to his left shoulder as he tried to grab her across the bed. Momentarily stunned, she dashed out and came back to the living room. He wasn't far behind.

The woman grabbed a bat from beside the front door.

"Get the hell away from me, you bastard!" she panted.

Suddenly seeing a real threat, he backed off carefully towards the kitchen with his hands in front of him to ward off any attacks.

"I hate you!" she screeched. "You pathetic excuse of a man. I should have ditched you when you killed my first husband. You are the reason I lost it all!" She started to advance on him. He backed up to the counter and found the knife holder. He yanked out the biggest one and flashed it in front of her. He knew she was a coward and he the more experienced one. She had never killed anyone, that was always his job. She did as he expected her to and started to back off.

They both offered insults and yelled at each other, blaming the other for the tragedy that was their lives as they circled each other around the dining room table—her with her bat, him with his knife.

The lightning had stopped and it began to rain. At first it was light, but quickly became a hard heavy rain bordering on hail. It beat against the roof—the perfect drumbeat to the violence inside. The mood turned calmly murderous. In the darkness, only portions of their face could be seen. As they moved slowly around the table, the hall light illuminated first his face fixed in hatred, then her face etched with malice.

The woman made the first move. She jumped over the short part of the table and swung the bat at the man's head. He raised his arm to try and block the impact, but it still glanced off his right ear, splitting the skin and making the remaining hair on his head crimson with his own blood.

She swung the bat back to hit him again but the man surged forward and pinned her against the peeling wallpaper. With his left hand that had the knife he pinned the old woman's arm to the wall and the other hand he grasped her throat. The mad look of murder flashed in his eyes.

The woman gasped for breath as she struggled against him, kicking and scratching his face. She got him between the legs and he dropped his grip on her throat as he pinned his legs together to hold himself from the pain his groin. The crack of the bat when it collided against his back could have been mistaken for another peal of thunder.

He crashed against the ground and waited through the pain for the next blow, but it didn't come. He looked up and saw the woman gasping, holding her throat, leaning against the bat. She saw him and with fear and malice in her eyes raised the bat again. He lunged again at her and with a move reminiscent of his old football days, caught her with his shoulder against her middle. She made an "oof" sound as the air was driven from her lungs. The next second, his knife sank easily into her left breast. He held her there, pinned by his shoulder as she trembled.

Blood began to pour down her once expensive blouse as she looked at him with pain, hatred, and terror in her eyes. She attempted to curse him but couldn't draw the breath, and with a feeble grasp she tried to pull his hand from the knife hilt.

He finally released her and watched as she slid down the wall gasping for breath. He grabbed the bat from her now limp grip and watched as she feebly drew the knife from her chest and sputtered on the floor. Rookie mistake, he thought. Never take the knife out. Blood filled her left lung making her cough and wheeze. The pain and fear that were present in her eyes did not mask the malice she felt for him.

She mouthed something unintelligible and her eyes closed for the last time.

He stood there for a while, disbelief and relief chasing each other in his head, but one thought kept at the fore: He needed to hide the body.

He glanced quickly around the house and looking past the front window he spotted the old rotten oak tree in the front yard. It was dark and no one was going to be out in this kind of downpour, he told himself as he lifted her dead body.

He didn't want to have her body exposed to the whole world, so he found an old blanket and wrapped the corpse into it, then he dragged the body out the front door and started to dig at the base of the tree. The rain had made the mud soft so the digging was easy, and after he had a hole deep enough, he shoved the body of the woman who had been his wife under the tree.

Once she was completely in, her body wrapped around some of the larger roots, he attempted to fill in the hole, but he knew it looked too fresh. Fortune blessed him, then, as a limb from the old oak crashed down from the tree and mostly obscuring the freshly dug grave.

Quickly, he ran inside and cleaned up the blood as well as he could—making sure to get the walls and floor. He examined the job. Some of it was soaked in, but it didn't look any worse than the rest of the stains in the house. Next, he dressed in new clothes and lifted the loose floorboards in the bedroom to reveal a suitcase. Inside the suitcase was several thousand dollars, a passport with an alias on it, and various other items that he might need for a sudden escape. The money wasn't enough to get out of the trouble she had put him in, but it would let him have a fresh start south of the border. He was thankful that she had never found out about it. He had always known that someday he would need to flee quickly—he always knew it would end in murder.

He checked the house for anything else he might need, but there was nothing else he wanted from this hated place. He left with his raincoat on, got into the car, and drove away without another glance.

Under the tree, intelligence stirred—a malevolent spark awoke. She looked around, and below her the ground opened and she saw the glowing red abyss that wished to give her her just reward. The spark struggled, though, against the pull of the abyss. She screamed the unholy wail of a banshee; she hated the injustice that the world had given her. She hated the man who had taken her from the world of the living. She reached out with her mind and found the life-force of the dying oak tree. She suckled against that life, clinging to it with all her might. The bark darkened and the few leaves left on the tree withered. She looked around at her surroundings; she could see just outside the tree and could feel the immediate ground where she sucked at the tree. She felt a familiar form, reached for it and found her own dead body. She wailed again at her misfortune and clung to the world of the living. She would get them, how dare they take her rightful place above them. But she was weak. She needed to regain strength, and then she would make them all pay. She latched onto the tree with every fiber of her will and slowly the red glow of the world below faded. Relief filled her and vengeance consumed her. She vowed that she would get him back. She would make him pay for killing her. She would make them all pay. Every loan shark, every lover who scorned her, and all the people that thought they were so much better than she was. Death was no longer a barrier to her. She could feel herself becoming stronger from the nourishment of the oak. She would take the light from their eyes. She would make them beg for her forgiveness and then she would take their very souls! She would make sure that no one ever laughed at her again. She smiled without form and settled in to wait for her revenge.

The man thought he heard a scream as he pulled out of the driveway but he sped down the road trying to get as much distance between him and the house. Several miles away, just as he started to feel like he was safe, he slid on the wet pavement and skidded over a bridge. He screamed as his car fell over the side and his head hit the steering wheel, leaving him dazed. The rushing water sealed his doors shut as he struggled feebly against the latch.

As the water filled his car, his last thought was that he deserved this and it was better this way—at least he wouldn't need to answer to the police.

The water rose above his head and he held his breath against the inevitable. As the lights dimmed in his eyes, he let out breath and involuntarily tried to breathe in again. The water he inhaled collapsed his lungs and shocked his body into lifelessness.

In the water a flicker of intelligence awoke, the flicker gazed around. He saw his body. He moaned in desperation and tried to rise, but felt heavy. He glanced down and saw to his horror a red abyss. He felt the pull of it and tried to struggle but to no avail. It sucked him down as he cried with despair.

CHAPTER ONE

Of course, there was no police investigation. The relief the neighbors felt when they heard that the old couple had abandoned the house was overwhelming. No one cared to find out what happened to the couple. The neighborhood felt that, finally, there would be a return to peace and tranquility.

The owner of the little house could find no one to sell or rent it to however, and the house fell into disrepair. Over the next couple years, the house was foreclosed on and condemned.

As for the old oak tree, it lost all remaining leaves and became dry and brittle while the trunk turned a black ash color. It stood like a sentinel in the front yard; branches dangling near the sidewalk, leaving anyone who passed by with the feeling that they would grab anyone who dared get close.

Several times, crews were called out to remove the tree or fix the house. Each time the crew grew paranoid and left the premises complaining that the house and the lot felt "wrong." No matter the crew, company, or amount of money promised by the bank to clean up the lot, no crew stayed very long. Perhaps long enough to setup and take a couple of whacks at the front porch before they felt a malevolence that chased them off. None of the crews would even go near the tree—and even when parking in the drive, they steered clear of it.

Children stopped going by the street that the house was on. Any playdates or gatherings would go around the house and it's warding tree, sometimes even to other streets just to be safe. Stories on how the tree was haunted began to pop up around the neighborhood. For a while teenage boys would dare their friends to see how long they could stand being close to the house before freaking out. No one lasted very long though, and the games petered out. The neighbors on either side moved out eventually as well, being finally overcome by the sheer hatred that emanated from that house and, as they referred to it, "that creepy tree."

The surrounding houses would be rented out by several tenants over the years, each lasting only a short time, maybe six months to two years before they would break lease and leave.

The house to the right went derelict and was eventually returned to the bank. Eventually, the bank renovated the home and put it on sale as a reclaimed house.

Finally, a man name Nathaniel Grey purchased this home.

Nathaniel had just finished signing papers to purchase this lovely three bedroom, two bath ranch in a quaint little suburb—just far enough from work that he didn't feel like he needed to go in every day, but close enough that if he did it wasn't a big deal. He felt proud of himself. When he was shopping for houses, this one had come up as a real steal. He was always on the market for a good deal and jumped at the opportunity to get in on a house that would be half his rent back in the city. He hadn't even gone inside the vacancy to check it out, just checking out the property from his car on a drive by. There was a condemned house next door, but he was sure that they would tear that down and get a good house built there fairly quickly. Then the property would skyrocket in value and he would be able to sell and get a real nice house in the country in six or seven years. He couldn't wipe the smile off his face.

Coming out of the real estate office, Nathaniel paid no mind to the obvious relief that the realtors showed as he finished signing. He was not aware of the fact that they had been trying to unload the house for a good three plus years. The bank was taking a loss on the place, but they figured that a loss was better than never unloading the property. They would be able to make that up in the next few properties that they sold off in better neighborhoods.

As he drove down the highway to his new home, he made all the arrangements for the moving company to bring his stuff from his one-bedroom apartment to the new house. He was proud of himself for getting cable, electricity, water, and trash setup within one day—ahhhh, the marvels of technology.

Nathaniel went to his new home and parked in *his* new driveway. God that felt good to say. HIS house. HIS drive way. HIS front yard. He gazed at the new domain. He took a look around and spotted the derelict house off to his left. It was an eye sore, for sure. It threatened to rain on his good mood, but he wasn't going to let that happen. He was sure it was only a matter of time before it was demo'ed.

His eye fell on the darkened oak tree in the front yard; he shivered. He looked back at his house and smiled—the cold feeling forgotten—and hurried inside.

Having the movers come and deliver all his stuff made him realize that "all" his stuff wasn't enough. He needed to go furniture shopping, soon. The house looked much sparser than his one-bedroom apartment had. There were entire rooms that had nothing in them. They looked so sad, and he was just the person to do something about it. A workout room in one spare and all his video games in the other. He smirked to himself. This was going to be great.

As he glanced around the living room, he liked the paint job and the carpet, but when he looked out the front window, he knew he was going to have to do something about the front yard. There was nothing going on there and it looked boring—it needed to be spruced up a bit. It was still early spring, though, maybe he would wait until summer to do something about the yard.

Over the days and weeks that followed, he settled into a rhythm with his work and home life. He was able to decorate the house and get a home office setup so he could work from home. It was a lot of money, but everything was setup to his liking. He all but ignored the house next door and for the most part everything was going well.

He loved his new life. He did what he wanted. He didn't have to talk to anyone. The neighbors kept to themselves, he could stay inside and play video games all day when not working, and even then he could work from home most days. They had even given up his office downtown to some new guy. They tried to act like it was some huge thing and that it didn't mean a thing, but Nathaniel was thrilled. It meant that there was even less reason to go into the office.

Things went well for a couple of months. Nathaniel was just starting to think about starting work on the front yard when things at work began to go downhill for him. He was getting behind in his work. The biggest part of the problem was corporate promoting that jerk Adam to project manager. Before, he had been a brown-nosing know it all, now he was micromanaging everything they did. There was no autonomy anymore. He kept inserting deadlines for stupid things like metrics on what he had done compared to other parts of the project, like that meant anything, trying to "maximize productivity," whatever the hell that was supposed to mean. All the additional bullshit that he was being told to do meant that the actual work he needed to do—crunching the numbers for the new expansion into the Norwest territory surrounding Spokane—was being bogged down. There was no reason for that. Nathaniel was sure it was just Adam trying to be the best new thing to suck up to the big wigs at Corporate, but that certainly wasn't making it easy for him.

Over the next few months, the workload just kept getting worse and worse. He now had standup meetings every morning that he had to teleconference into in order to meet quotas and status reports due at the end of every week. It was nearly as bad as being in the office. That jack-ass Adam was running them ragged and the idiot didn't see that he was getting no result from it.

In fact, he was actually starting to drive everyone off. Cheryl had already quit and was working for another marketing firm. Kyle and Mitch were both actively looking for work and the rest were hunkering down to weather the Adam storm. There was a lot of grumbling from pretty much everyone. Nathaniel was glad that he didn't have to go in, otherwise he might just sock Adam in his brownnosing little mouth. He tried to bring it up to management and he was professional and polite while trying to point out that there was no value added to Adam's behavior, but management sided with Adam as the team lead, or merely offered placating words with no commitment to do anything about it.

The thing was, how was he going to leave the company? He had just bought a house and had debt coming out of his ears that he needed to pay off. He wasn't going to quit now that he was actually doing what he wanted. So, he tried to hunker down for the long haul. Leads never stick around for any length of time anyway, he told himself. So, he kept going. The market research for Spokane was finally finished—although it was three weeks overdue and he kept hearing about that. He had even put in extra hours to try and get it in on time. But it didn't matter, upper management was breathing down his neck anyway, and Adam was their golden child. He hated the way Adam spoke to him, like a goddamn six-year old. What was he supposed to do, put in eighty hour weeks just so he could do all the extra work that that idiot wanted? He started dreading logging in every morning. This was supposed to be a good job with flexible hours and the ability to avoid the normal office bullshit that haunted work.

Nathaniel was becoming bitter at his boss and the job. The next job they had him working on, required him to come in to the office in order to "collaborate" with the other people on the team. He got pulled into H.R. once for yelling at Kyle for being an idiot and was put on a P.I.P (Performance Improvement Plan) to improve his attitude. It wasn't even Kyle's fault, he was just so mad at Adam that he blew up without thinking. What a load of crap.

After one particularly infuriating day, Nathaniel determined he needed to take a walk—to get away from his computer, his home office, and the ridiculous conference call he had just ended. He grabbed his shoes and slammed the front door behind him as he left. He looked morosely around his yard. With the extra workload he'd been forced to endure his yard looked terrible. He hadn't gotten around to installing the sprinkler system and he hadn't wanted to have someone do it for him. The grass was yellowed and patchy, which certainly didn't improve his disposition.

He looked next door at the derelict house that was *still* an eye sore for him. He'd found out from a neighborhood kid that the house had been like that for as long as anyone could remember. It sounded like it wasn't going to be restored or torn down any time soon. He hated that house almost as much as he hated Adam. In his anger and frustration, he had cut off all his friends, claiming workload. He had yelled at his brother and now no one from the family was talking to him.

He caught sight of the tree, its leafless black bark seeming to glare at him. He glared back. "Fuck off." he barked at the tree. He immediately felt foolish for talking to a tree, but it felt good to yell.

He gave the tree the finger and started walking the block.

She woke. Anger and resentment like she hadn't felt in a long time came from close by. The feelings made her hungry and alive again. No one came down this road anymore, she thought bitterly. Everyone stayed away from this place; they didn't like the feeling it radiated, they said. She sensed a new presence, but somehow it was familiar to her. She mulled it over and over in her mind. What felt so familiar about the resentment? It had been a while since she'd felt any emotion other than unmiti-

gated hatred for the living and their ability to walk around freely while she was locked in this sickly, worn down tree.

The resentment she felt so close and so strong began to diminish, moving farther and farther away. Then, suddenly, something clicked. Her husband! It had to be him. Who else would direct such anger at her? There was no one that knew that she was down here, except him. That insolent prick had not been back for some time. It had to be him. She felt around frantically, trying to feel his anger again. He was getting away! She was going to lose him. She wanted so badly to exact her vengeance on him. She would, she told herself, and she would get him.

Nathaniel wandered down the road fuming to himself about the conference call from the Florida office. He spent several hours trying to convince the brainless drones that a hybrid pear and apple product would be a good venture for them to buy into based on the data that he had been pulling for the last several weeks. They finally agreed to look over the numbers and get back to him, but he knew that was as good as a no. He would never hear about it and all his hard work would go to nothing.

Nathaniel felt a sudden chill, like a rabid dog was breathing down his neck. He turned in spite of himself. There was something there, he knew it, but he saw nothing. Just that old decrepit tree.

His eyes locked on the old oak tree. It seemed ... angry at him? What was he saying, trees don't have feelings, he reminded himself. He shook his head trying to clear the impression that a tree wanted to kill him. He almost apologized to the thing for swearing at it, but surely a tree couldn't need an apology, right? His mouth opened and he started to say sorry, but he shook himself and walked away, shaking his head. He just needed to get away from the tree for the moment and so he turned the corner up the next block.

Then, suddenly, he heard a loud, ear-piercing wail. It was shrill and evil and he felt it in his bones. He wanted to run, far and fast but he couldn't. Somehow, he knew where it came from.

His heart turned to stone in his chest as he turned and peered around the corner and saw a hooded figure scraping and clawing out of the bark of the tree.

For a moment, he was too stunned to move. He watched in horror as it came free of the old oak tree.

Then, he came to his senses and he was off like a shot. He raced down the sidewalk and skidded as he turned another corner, nearly falling on a patch of gravel that had spilled from the yard next to it. He heard the wail getting closer and he risked a glance back. The creature was catching up to him. It was horrible to look at. There was only half a body, the lower half of the body trailed off into some kind of shroud. The only well-defined parts were the hands, which were extended in a clawed posture towards him. Nathaniel saw that where the eyes should have been there were indents instead and the mouth was just a gaping hole. The whole thing seemed to be bound up in some kind of sheet or something.

He picked up the pace. He sprinted faster than he had ran in his life. His heart pounding against his chest like it was trying to jump ahead of him still. He ran blindly, not knowing where he was going. He turned corners and dashed down side-walks trying to escape the nightmare that was screaming after him. He recognized one of the streets. It was the one he lived on—he'd run in a gi-ant circle.

He raced as fast as he could down his street, seeing his house in the distance. The creature screamed more urgently as if frustrated it hadn't caught up with him. Nathaniel feared that he could-n't go much further, his lungs ached, his legs were on fire, and his heart felt like it was going to explode in his chest. With one last burst of adrenaline, he managed to race down his street, into his house, and slam the door behind him. Whatever was chasing him ran headlong into house and the house shud-dered from the force of the blast.

The ghoul banged on the door, screaming an unholy wail as it tried to get in. Nathaniel locked the deadbolt behind him. He looked at the window as the demented being scraped and pounded and rattled the handle. He dry heaved, bending over with his mouth open wide trying and expel anything in his stomach. What was he going to do? He took solace knowing that, for now, the thing couldn't seem to get past his door. He had thankfully locked the dead bolt.

He feared that the creature might be able to reason out another entrance, so he hurried as best he could to the other doors and windows making sure all were locked and safe. He quickly made his way to the living room. The banging had stopped and once or twice he had seen the ghost, or ghoul or whatever it was, circling the house looking for a way in. He was safe for the moment—he hoped.

He sat down in his chair by the fireplace and wept in his hands. What was that thing? What did it want from him? He heard a rage-filled scream of triumph from the roof and his heart sank to his shoes. He scrambled to get up and shove something in front of the fireplace but before he could, the horrible creature disgorged itself from the chimney. It scanned the room and its gaze settled on Nathaniel.

The thing leapt at him and grabbed him by the throat.

She had him! She had the dirty scumbag that had killed her and left her to rot. She squeezed on his throat with ecstasy. She wanted to feel him. Feel his last breath. She drew closer while he struggled in her grasp. Something started to happen to her as she held him. Her essence began pouring into him. She began to feel his pain—the torment and terror that he was feeling. It was intoxicating. It was exhilarating. It was like living again!

She gave herself up completely to him now, coming in through his mouth and nose, through his ears and tear ducts. She squeezed herself through the pores in his face and arms. She released her grip on his neck and focused on inhabiting this new host. The man's arms went to his neck. He was still unable to breathe even after she let go. Oh, she loved the racing heartbeat, the lungs clawing desperately for air, the adrenaline pumping through the blood stream as she filled every part of him. The last wisps of her essence came into the man and she began to take stock of herself. She could feel herself pulled down to the ground as the man was finally able to breath and collapsed on the floor coughing and sputtering. She felt the lungs as they heaved with fresh air, refilling the blood vessels with life. She didn't wait long. She would tear her husband's mind apart with her own hands and then see what she was left with. She tore at his mind and was rewarded with an assault of memories. But these memories were not of her old husband! This wasn't him! This was someone else. No. NO. NO! She screamed and heard the man echo with his own lungs. She threw herself to the ground and felt the man's body crumple to the floor.

Well, this is interesting. She seemed to be able to move this body with her own will, over-riding his. An evil grin spread across her face and she was pleased to see that it was mimicked on the face of her new host. It all became suddenly quite clear how she would take vengeance on those who slighted her. She would use this pitiful excuse for a man and make him serve her to carry on her vengeful tirade against the living.

Nathaniel stopped shuddering and slowly picked himself up. He stood where he was and carefully turned himself around. What new Hell is this, he wondered. He shrugged his shoulders and rotated his arms. He made his way to the bathroom to look at himself. Taking a look in the mirror he saw a nasty lump forming on the right side of his head and blood was still streaming down his cheek from the fall. A smile that he could not remove from his face kept grinning back at him and a low throaty laugh escaped his lips. He tried to pull back but found he couldn't. He tried to turn his head but it wouldn't budge. His eyes widened in terror as he tried to move anything, or do anything in order to regain control. He managed to lift his arm to his face and felt fury and anger. His arm snapped down to his side and he felt himself slam down onto the counter. The impact knocked the wind out of him and he reeled against the back wall, putting a hole in it.

He realized he no longer had control over his own body. The creature had total authority now. He tried to whimper but no sound came out.

CHAPTER TWO

The next morning, a phone call woke Nathaniel—the morning status call. His head was splitting and his teeth felt loose in his head. He couldn't think straight as he fumbled around in his pockets for his phone. He reached it, nearly dropped it, and answered the call.

"Thanks for joining us this morning," came the sarcastic voice from the other side.

"Sorry, Adam," Nathaniel croaked.

"Are you sick or something? You sound like death." A smatter of laughter from other disembodied voices accompanied the comment.

"No, I just…" Nathaniel trailed of—what had happened? He couldn't remember. "Look, I'm sorry, I'm gonna have to take a sick day today." And without waiting for a reply, he shut off his phone. Man, he felt like crap. He was sore and beat up—had he been drinking? No, there wasn't even any booze in the house right now.

He wandered over to the mirror in the bathroom, all the while trying to figure out what happened last night. His face was a mess. He had a huge lump on the right side of his head and it looked like he'd gotten a black eye. He didn't know what to think but he did know one thing; he needed a shower. It smelled like he had pissed himself last night.

He took a deep breath, which sent him into a coughing fit. He must have been running hard last night. He imagined that he must have been running away from whoever did this to him. Too bad I didn't get away in time, he rued. He tried to remember anything about his assailant, but the face eluded him.

Still puzzling over it, he stripped down, peeling off his clothes and stepping into the shower. He had woken up in the living room wearing yesterday's clothes and he needed to get fresh. He hoped the shower would relieve some of the pain in his head too.

He might even go to the hospital if it didn't look better before long. It was a statement on how bad he felt. He had a high deductible and with everything going on, he didn't have the money at the moment.

Nathaniel scrubbed his face and washed his hair. The lump on his head was really painful, but he noticed that it didn't bleed when he washed it. He gazed at the steam that rose from the hot water. *Steam.* The steam was familiar somehow ... trailing mist, fog, or...

The memory he'd been blocking out suddenly rushed back to him. That hideous spirit from the night before! That evil laugh, the banshee screams, the eyeless face with the hands choking him and then… No, it couldn't have happened. He finished washing himself and threw on some new clothes. He was going to the hospital right now.

As he approached the door, however, his body froze. He legs spun him around and sat down in his armchair. His head snapped back and forth and he shook his finger at himself like some kind of admonishment.

He tried for the door again. This time, his hand reached up and smacked his face. He legs jerked out from under him and his arms threw him to the ground. He was powerless to get up or move. His mouth spoke, but it wasn't his own voice that came to him, it was shrill and high-pitched with a whispering note to it.

"No, pet. No running away now."

He whimpered.

"Who... what are you?"

"It doesn't matter, pet. You just be a good boy and everything will be fine." With this, a cackle came from his lips.

"You ... you can't do this," he pleaded.

His mouth gave a small half smile. *"Of course I can. I can do anything I want."* For punctuation his arm reached up and caressed his face, fingernails gently scratching on his stubble. His hand reached down and grabbed his dick, giving it one or two good tugs. Then, suddenly, he reached up and punched himself hard in the gut. He oofed as the wind was knocked out of him.

He curled into a ball and cried.

The more time that passed, the more the presence in his body seemed to take control. In the beginning, he could do some things by himself. He was not able to leave the house at all, but he could use the bathroom or cook on his own. He was sure that the presence holding him captive was a *she*. She liked to call him pet, and even rewarded him when he did something she deemed as "good." She liked different things than he did to eat, but he found that she didn't know how to cook very well. So, while he cooked, she would leave him alone.

She also seemed interested in the difference in physiology between man and woman and often when watching Nathaniel trying to do something, would take control of his body and do it for herself. This ended disastrously for Nathaniel the first time she peed standing up. Piss went everywhere and she became furious. She forced him to march over to the kitchen and grab the nearest knife. He could only watch as his own hand hovered over various points of his body, as if she was not sure where to cut first. His hand closed in on his chest and he scored three cuts into his left breast. She seemed to enjoy it as he screamed in pain. Afterward, she let him bandage himself up. She had an interest in keeping him healthy, if not sane.

Anytime Nathaniel attempted to assert control when she was doing something, it always ended badly. Maybe not with a knife to his chest, but him slamming his head into the wall or lighting some part of him on fire. The latter had terrified him so much that he did not dare struggle again.

The only time that he had to himself was cooking or when he did other menial tasks. She decided that she was too good for house work and left him to it. However, at the drop of a hat she could force him to go off and do something else. He learned to submit immediately to these situations.

She was pleased. This was working out very well. She was feeling all the joys of living again. She tasted food through his tongue, felt blood race through his body as he moved. She even enjoyed using the bathroom, she admitted to herself. It was wonderful. She had made him quit his wretched job in order to take full care of her. That had happened the second time those imbeciles from work called. How dare they wake her from her beauty sleep. She laughed when he tried to stop her and then she punished him for the attempt. You have to train dogs to do as you wish, otherwise they run amok, she told herself.

Living again was wonderful, though. But living as a man was...unusual—the meaty hands, the lumbering gait. She was not beautiful anymore, which angered her, and she took out her frustration on her pet. He did have a function though; he had skills that she did not and it was pleasant to not concern herself with doing the work around the house.

She was strengthening now, being in a new host. She had been afraid that she would be tied to that dead piece of wood her body was buried under forever. Luckily, that did not seem to be the case. She was in full flush again, doing as her whims dictated. She'd almost forgotten about her desire for vengeance and spite, but not entirely. She was merely biding her time until something occurred and pointed her in the right direction.

She decided to take a walk. She'd been cooped up in this poor excuse for a house too long. It would do her good to see the world, even if it was through his eyes.

He stepped outside for the first time in a long time. A chill wind blew, making him shiver. Spring had not dissipated all the cold from the air yet. He took a look around. His yard was overgrown and in desperate need of mowing. There were weeds growing in the driveway. His car had bird crap on it and the whole thing looked of disuse. He looked over at the tree and gave an involuntary shudder as he remembered her clawing out of it.

She moved him across the yard until he came to a spot right behind the tree. A large limb lay in front of him. She made him pick it up and move it aside. He didn't understand what she was doing but he didn't resist.

Below the limb was regular dirt and he dug for a few inches until his hand snagged on something not earth. He cleared away the debris and found an old rotten blanket. He suspected what might be under it and recoiled at the thought. He scrambled back but was halted just a few feet away. He waited for the blow to come—for his hand to grab a rock or something and attack him with it—but it didn't. He could only assume it was because they were outside and she worried that someone might see.

Slowly and with measured movements, he made his way back to the blanket buried under the tree. He grabbed it and ripped it easily as the rotten substance crumbled in his hands. He looked down in disgust at the corpse below him. The face was sunken with hair sticking out of it. He could see the head and part of the neck, but he would have to uncover it to find more. Suddenly, he heard sounds from up the street. Hastily, he recovered the head with the cloth and reburied it. He grabbed the branch that had been over the spot and threw it back. He tried to stand up, but fell over and landed face down on the ground.

From overhead, he heard derisive laughter.

His eyes snapped open and his head turned to see three teenage girls walking towards him laughing at his stumble. The first girl was tall but young—maybe fourteen or fifteen years old. She had blond hair tied in a ponytail with high cheekbones and a slim nose that highlighted her bright blue eyes. Her mouth had a pouty quality as she laughed, making her look cruel but beautiful. The second girl was slightly shorter with chestnut hair falling past her shoulders. Her dark eyes and more prominent nose gave her an adult look, but the backpack told otherwise. Her clothes gave her the impression of wealth. The third girl, also with chestnut hair, had the same brown eyes as the shorter girl, but she was obviously younger. She wasn't laughing.

"You all right, sir?" she inquired as she proffered her hand.

His hand pushed the girl's away. "I'm fine," he grunted. He tried to get up but his legs were still caught in the branch and he fell down again.

The younger girl attempted to help, but the older girls snapped at her. "Get off him, Vicky."

"Yeah, let the boozer get himself home," the other giggled.

"Sorry, sir, I gotta go," Vicky said. The other two girls pulled her along laughing and mocking the younger girl.

Those two trollops just sealed their death note, she fumed. She got to her feet; she wanted to go after them right now, but her old patience held. She followed them at a distance until she saw them head into a house a block down the road. She would wait. It was just fine. She would wait until they came out and then she would get them. She was very good at waiting.

CHAPTER THREE

It rained that afternoon. A torrential downpour that soaked everything and left puddles of water everywhere. Hidden behind a fence, Nathaniel dripped, miserable and cold. His body would not let him go home or dry off. His eyes kept watching the house where the three girls had gone. His legs ached from standing, and he knew that whatever she was planning; it wasn't good.

Afternoon turned into evening. She couldn't control the shivering of her pet but that didn't matter. She would catch these miscreants and make them pay. Finally the door opened. The two older girls stepped out of the house and started down the walk. Perfect. She tailed them until they were out of the light, then she rushed them. The first girl, the one with the blond hair, barely had time to turn and look before a stout stick walloped her along the side of her head. She went down in a satisfying heap. The brunette started to scream and run, but was tripped as the club came down to sweep her off her feet.

Oh, the exhilaration! She had never killed someone before. It was exciting, so empowering. She grabbed the brunette by the hair and pulled her over to where the blond laid sprawled on the ground; she was just starting

Chapter Three

to stir. She took the blond in her other hand—it was surprising how strong she was in this host. It was delicious. She marched the girls back to the scene of their crime.

Nathaniel watched horrified as his hands gripped the brunette by the roots of her hair and the other by her neck. Both whimpered and tried to get away, but his hands were like vice grips. There was no way they could escape. His feet marched back towards the tree.

"Please, stop!"

"Please, mister. We're sorry!"

"Please don't."

"Help!" The girls cried as his feet shuffled forward. He tried so hard to break free of the control of the demon inside him. His mind echoed the frightened call of the girls. What was going to happen? What was she making him do? It was torture. His hand clamped down on the blond. He heard his voice hiss, "Be quiet or I strangle her."

The girls submitted and walked down the darkened street whimpering and sobbing.

Nathaniel hated himself. How could he be so weak? He had no control, no ability to help these girls—or himself. His eyes caught sight of the oak tree that she was once buried under. What was she planning for these girls?

They approached the tree, closer and closer. The girls must have sensed that something unthinkable was about to happen because they began, with renewed effort, to struggle, trying to kick and scratch their way out.

Nathaniel felt the kicks to his legs and felt the cuts on his arms ooze blood, but he couldn't even scream out. His voice croaked, "Stop! Or it will be worse for you." His arms rammed the two girls' heads together dazing them and causing them to stumble.

Finally, they reached the tree. His eyes scanned the area, looking for what he did not know. His eyes spotted a puddle right in front of the tree. No, he thought. No, no, no, don't do this, he tried to say.

"Kneel, and apologize, you wretched things," his voice hissed. He brought them to their knees.

"I'm sorry, I'm so sorry, please don't hurt me," the blond said.

"We didn't mean to hurt your feelings, please let us go," said the other.

His mouth formed an evil smile. "Oh. I'll let you go," his voice said in a silky tone. He felt the girls relax a bit in his hands and suddenly with all the force his body could muster he slammed their faces in the water.

The girls thrashed on the sidewalk as they struggled for breath. He watched, horrified as his body forced their heads under farther and farther into the muddy water. Everything was moving in slow motion.

"STOP!" he tried to cry out, but no matter how hard he tried, his arms would not move, his mouth never let go of that maniacal grin.

Ten seconds passed, twenty seconds, thirty seconds.

The brunette stopped struggling first. Her hands clawed the pavement one last feeble time and her body stopped moving. The blond struggled for a moment longer, arms flailing, legs kicking feebly.

Finally her body stopped resisting and succumbed to the water. His arms held them down for a full five minutes after the girls stopped struggling; their wet hair matted to the back of their heads.

His arms eventually pulled them out of the water. Their mouths were open but their eyes were closed. The color had already drained from their faces.

She smiled in satisfaction. What a wonderful feeling. She'd had total control over those stupid little wretches. She reminisced on how they tried to escape. How they begged. How they had thrashed in the water. Never had she felt more alive. Not even when she was in her own body had she felt this empowered—this strong.

It was intoxicating.

Now she just had to clean up. She smirked. No one had been in her old home for years. No one even liked approaching it.

She dragged the bodies up the weed infested yard into the rotten old house. She threw the bodies into the closet in the spare bedroom. Never had she had the experience of killing someone herself—it had always been her lazy oaf of a husband who did the dirty work when they pulled any job. She never appreciated how many emotions could run through her, from fear of failure to exhilaration and, yes, even orgasm. She was heady, hot and bothered. Not that she could do anything about it.

She turned in to the bathroom and

rubbed the grime off the mirror to look at her pet properly. He wasn't bad looking after all. Oh, but it wouldn't do for her to just satisfy herself. Always after she had pulled a job, they had consummated the completion with a dance and sex. But there was no one to dance with...

Her face crooked in a smirk.

She knew what she would do. She started to cackle madly as the rain lashed the condemned house.

CHAPTER FOUR

Nathaniel was still stunned and appalled. He couldn't comprehend the actions his body had taken—all he could do was whimper internally. She wouldn't even let him cry properly.

Those poor girls. Now they were in that wretched house next door, thrown into a closet. The sight of their tangled limbs and dead eyes would haunt him for the rest of his life; he knew it. His body had been moving about the house for a while now, looking for what he did not know. He had been through the garage, the shed, and a couple of other places. The more places he went, the more agitated the presence seemed to get. His mind barely registered it though. He was still reeling from the horror of the night.

In the kitchen his hands picked up a shovel. He went back out into the rain and approached the old oak tree. He began to dig. What now, he despaired. He recognized the place that they were digging. It was the place that he had been before. Her body was under there. He wondered despondently whether he would be burying her in a better place or moving her body for some other reason. He supposed it didn't matter. His life was effectively over now. She was his only motivator now. She had made that amply clear the last few hours.

At first the digging was slow and careful as the shovel made cautious holes around the body. The rain seemed to have stopped and he kept at it. As it got later and later, the digging became faster and more careless. The result was that the top half of the body was very carefully preserved while the legs and waist were destroyed. He was breathing hard from the exertion she was forcing on him. His arms burned and his back was killing him.

His body stopped digging for a moment and he leaned on the shovel. His arms then threw the shovel away and began to pull on the body, bringing it out of the ground.

Oh God, he thought. He was taking it out of the ground. It was so foul and disgusting—worms scurried away from the body as his arms yanked and pulled. He heard a sloppy rip and the legs tore away from the rest of the body. He fell backwards with the corpse on top of him. His stomach reeled. He nearly threw up but she stopped him.

He stood up and his body picked up the woman's corpse. Grunting with the effort of it, he managed to keep the body up. Entrails hung from it, swinging, wrapping and unwrapping around his legs. The head kept falling back with the jaw dropped open. He was repulsed when his hand pulled the head and put it on his shoulder. His mouth started to hum an old tune and he began to dance with it. At first he only swung back and forth rocking with the molding corpse. Eventually, he started to move around more. His legs picked out a pattern that he wasn't familiar with. His mouth hummed and sang the tune; the Claire de Lune, he realized.

In his mind, he stopped thinking entirely. No thoughts could process in his head. He was too repulsed to think.

As they moved about the yard, the revulsion and nausea gave way to anger. Anger at the way he was being treated. Anger at his lack of control. Anger at her using him to kill those girls. Anger at the injustice. Anger that he was now a murderer.

Along with the anger came disgust. Disgust for her and her macabre dance—for her control. He hated her. He hated her so much he couldn't take it anymore. He started to fight again. With every particle of his being he fought. He wanted her out! Out of his body, out of his life! He was going to get her out of him if it was the last thing he ever did.

His legs stopped moving. He pried his arms away from the dead thing that used to be this vile woman. Straining with his whole being, he thrust the corpse from him, causing it to land in the mud near the hole it came from. She tried to reassert control over him again, but it wasn't enough. He was too enraged, too consumed with hatred for the way she had ruined his life and committed those crimes with his body. There was no fear. There was no compromise.

He screamed, "GET OUT!"

He started to push. On what he couldn't even begin to tell, but he pushed. He pushed and pushed. Slowly the mist began to reappear. She began to seep through his pores, out of his mouth, out of every cut and laceration. Suddenly, the wraith was there in front of him, trying to get back in, trying to hold him in her deadly embrace. There she was. That hated thing.

"You have destroyed me!" he shouted. She screamed in response. She tried to grab him again but shrieked in pain and retreated. Seeing her in pain gave him vicious pleasure. He grabbed at her this time. She retreated again. He rushed at her and this time the wraith leaped back. She looked around as she dodged him and spotting the tree she dove into the roots and was absorbed by them.

Nathaniel stood there heaving. There was no joy in his eyes. Yes, she was out of his head, but his fingerprints were still on those bodies. He would still be tried for their murder. It would still be him trying to tell a jury that he had been possessed by an old woman. He would be lucky to get put into the looney bin instead of prison. It wasn't fair; it wasn't right! Oh, he hated her. He wanted to hurt her, kill her. His mind spun trying to find a way to exact vengeance. What would kill her? He would never be able to catch her, he realized. And if he cut down the tree she would merely find another host to possess. No, he wouldn't allow her to hurt anyone else ever again. He would hunt her forever, he would hurt her forever. A thought snapped into his mind: if she was the spirit of that woman, then he could do something, he would torment her till the end of days.

He raced back to his own house. No time for letters or notes, he had to be quick or she might get away. He grabbed a rope from the garage and raced back outside. He could still feel her in the tree. Good, he thought grimly to himself.

He began to mutter under his breath. "I'm gonna make you pay, bitch. You'll never get away. You're gonna regret what you did tonight." He tied a quick slip knot around one end and started to climb the tree.

She was exhausted. What just happened? One moment she was ruling on high, then she was almost destroyed by her pet!? She could still sense his hatred. It was searing and painful; the first painful thing she had experienced since she died. How the hell had he done that? She was forced to retreat into her asylum and she watched him warily. He raced back into his house. She had the limited senses of the tree again, and couldn't feel what was going on. A minute, two, ticked by and she felt she was safe again. She began to plot. She would take another host. She would kill this man, this usurper who would dare throw her off like dirty laundry.

Then she felt him again. He was coming towards her. Stupid man, she thought. He can't get me in here. She felt as he started to climb the tree. Anger was replaced by confusion.

What is he doing?

He made sure that he was high enough that his feet would never reach the ground. He tied off to a major limb, made sure that it wouldn't break and with the vengeful hatred of a man used for horrible things, he jumped off.

A fiery spark awoke. Anger fueled intelligence stirred as the man awoke. He looked around and saw two things: First, a woman, or at least what looked like a woman. She was decayed with time and looking away from him. From his angle he could see her distended features, her over extended mouth, her too long fingernails. She looked like a banshee from an Irish tale. He paused for a second and then recognition lit his intelligence. It was her! The hated one, the enemy, the one he would punish for all time. A deep red glow with fire licking the sides was the second thing he saw.

The abyss was back! She held on to the tree for all she was worth. Then she heard a blaze above her. She turned slowly and as her eyes lit upon the man she had possessed, she wailed an unholy scream. There he was, her pet, but he was hovering above her and he looked like a demon of Hell. He was glowing a deep crimson, his eyes spewing fire, his mouth an angry snarl with teeth sharpened. As she struggled to hang on, he continued to change. His hands became talons. A tail extended from behind him and his feet changed to hooves. The void didn't seem to bother him as it did her. He focused on her for a brief second, then launched at her. She didn't have time to react as he sped towards her. As he grabbed her by the throat, caustic immolation seared her neck. It was as if a car battery had burst into flame below her chin tearing at the very essence or her being. He collided with her; an experience akin to taking an acid bath. He roared in triumph echoing her scream of agony and despair. The furnace below beckoned flaring with heat. He focused that heat, and thrust it upwards into the host to purge it of all the evil that was hiding in its bark. Then with a wide eyed malevolent grin he sped downward into the abyss, his new home, to torment the hated one for all time.

In the predawn hours of the first day of summer the old oak erupted in a column of fire; burning from the inside out. At first the neighbors were too afraid to do anything. First, because there was a crazy man yelling, but more because no one would go near that tree. It was safer to stay inside, they all knew. The air of malevolence on the street was palpable.

Finally, 911 was notified. No one ever claimed to have called the fire department but they came anyway. By the time they arrived however, burning embers were all that remained of the sinister oak.

Over the next two days, several bodies were found on the premises. Two teenage girls from the neighborhood were found in a closet of the condemned property. A set of dental records were needed to confirm the identity of Nathaniel Grey and another body, burned beyond recognition, was also recovered.

The investigation concluded that Nathaniel Grey had murdered two teenage girls and possibly one other person and then tied himself to a tree and burned it. Testimony was given from many in the neighborhood that the man Nathaniel had been a loner, the type to do something so terrible. When questioned about why the condemned house still stood when several orders had been issued for its demolition, neither the construction crews nor the neighbors would comment.

The most compelling testimony of the ordeal came from a young teenager named Vicky. Her account of the fearful look in the man's eyes when he had fallen and the malice that he had spoken to her sister and her friend before they were murdered, her tearful breakdown on the stand when she testified that she had tried to warn them not to go back out that night brought silence to the court. The judge ordered the building demolished and all traces of the scene to be removed.

It took two more banks and three more years to sell the land. Eventually the lawsuit that was brought up against the produce chain that Nathaniel Grey worked at was settled out of court. The property of the scene of the crime would be purchased by Grocers Champions and a memorial would be erected to the two teenage girls who were so senselessly murdered there. Additionally, a man, Adam Zabliss, was to be fired for failing to communicate effectively with HR regarding Mr. Gray. A statement that Grocers Champions made to the press: "Any person so unbalanced that they are capable of such gruesome acts would have exhibited indicators that our management staff have been trained to pick up on."

Now nearly eighteen, Vicky Forsythe approved the design for the memorial and had overseen its construction. After the paint had dried and the sod had been laid, it was quite lovely; a sidewalk in the middle of the plot led to an open pavilion where, at the moment, a group of young girls were being taught self-defense. Vicky didn't join them just yet. Two paces to the left and about five paces in from the street was a patch of ground that just wouldn't take green. She went and stood on it. She knew what had stood here before. The tree that had scared everyone on the street. Now she didn't feel scared, she felt calm and much more grown up.

Vicky closed her eyes and let her thoughts drift. For just a moment the world was lost and she felt hot, like an oven door had been opened just in front of her. A thought more powerful than any others came to her in her drifting. "*Retribution is being delivered, gentle one.*" The presence faded, but the smile on her lips remained as she joined the girls at the pavilion to start the lesson.

Marvin Visher is from Aurora, Colorado where he still lives with his wife and son.

Made in the USA
San Bernardino, CA
04 June 2016